The Regimarilla from Regimarazz

The Regimarilla From Regimarazz

Penny Higgins

"Editor's Choice Award by The National Library Of Poetry 1995"

ReadersMagnet, LLC

The Regimarilla from Regimarazz

Published in the United States of America
ISBN Paperback: 978-1-954371-08-8
ISBN Hardback: 978-1-955603-19-5
ISBN eBook: 978-1-954371-09-5

ReadersMagnet, LLC
10620 Treena Street, Suite 230 | San Diego, California, 92131 USA
1.619.354.2643 | www.readersmagnet.com

Cover design by Ericka Obando
Interior design by Shemaryl Tampus
Illustrated by Jebb Impok

On the edge of the small town of Regimarazz
Lives a King in a palace. King Regi has
Six million soldiers, his life to protect.
He has six million dollars! (He's
sure that's correct).
He owns six million Zerkzeez
for his soldiers to ride.
The soldiers and Zerkzeez all hurry and hide
From the Regimarilla, a bear like beast
Who lives on the far side of town, in the east.

The Regimarilla has long shaggy hair,
And huge sharp fang teeth that
could certainly scare
A soldier, or zerkzeez, or even the king,
Who isn't afraid of most anything.
A Regimarilla! A monster so big;
He's as big as an elephant, two dogs and a pig,
A couple of cows and one large horse!
(That may be an exaggeration, of course.)
He's mean as a lion and sly as a fox!
However, he has had a few hard knocks.
But he's so unkind, and bad tempered too!
So everyone runs when he comes into view.

Now Regimarillas have lately been scarce,
For all but one beast were caught in big snares.
They were caught by the king of Regimarazz
And the six million soldiers
and Zerkzeez he has.
They were tangled and tied
and shipped far away
To the country of Tinsu, in the town of Torkay.
One Regimarilla is clearly enough
Since he acts so mean, and he sounds so gruff!

Still, the Rilla gets lonely! He longs for a friend.
If not a Rilla, then maybe a Zend?
A Zend, though he isn't a Rilla, should do
With his wagging tail, and his cute ears too!
But the Zend wouldn't "friend" the Rilla because
Of the mean, ugly things he so often does.
The Zend would not stay. He would not play
With the Rilla. He would just run away.
The king and his men entertain quite a lot.
The Regimarilla? OH NO he does not!
He never has company, and that's really sad.
Although the Rilla is mean, he's not bad...

Not REALLY bad, and we ALL, it is true,
Need a friend, a companion, someone to talk to.
When King Regi, the wise king,
heard the dilemma
He took half his soldiers, and his wife, Emma,
And went to consult the mean beast of a bear
With his sharp fang teeth and
his long shaggy hair,
And his very loud **growl**. Oh,
the king had no fear
With his wife Emma and his soldiers all near!

ROAR!

Do your think when the king
knocked on the door
The Regimarilla gave a big ***ROARRR?***
Did he rant? Did he rave at the king and his wife
And the soldiers? Did he threaten their life?

NO! He actually laughed and giggled with glee.
He invited them in and offered them tea
And cookies and ice cream, and promised to be
The most pleasant beast in the country of Zee.

The king saw a positive change come about,
So he called for a truce, and
brought his band out.
They laughed and they talked
the whole night through,
And the king knew exactly what he must do.

Do you know what he did?
Can you possibly guess?
Do you know how the wise king
straightened the mess?

Yes! He ordered a Rilla named Milly be sent
Back to Regimarazz in the land of Zent.

Now the Rilla and Milly and the King and his wife
Are living a happy, contented Life.
Though sometimes problems
come up now and then
They solve them together and are happy again.

Do you know someone who is hurting or sad,
Or is mean? They might really be glad
If you, or someone would happily lend
A hand, or a smile, or would just be a friend.

10620 Treena Street, Suite 230
San Diego, California,
CA 92131 USA
www.readersmagnet.com
1.619.354.2643

www.ingramcontent.com/pod-product-compliance
Ingram Content Group UK Ltd.
Pitfield, Milton Keynes, MK11 3LW, UK
UKHW062002290726
14090UKWH00021B/1346

9 781954 371088